OONGA BOONGA

OONGA BOONGA

by Frieda Wishinsky

Pictures by Suçie Stevenson

Little, Brown and Company
Boston Toronto London

FIRST EDITION

Library of Congress Cataloging-in-Publication Data

Wishinsky, Frieda.
Oonga boonga/by Frieda Wishinsky; pictures by Suçie Stevenson.
p.   cm.
Summary: Big brother Daniel seems to have just the right touch
when it comes to making Baby Louise stop crying.
ISBN 0-316-94872-1
[1. Babies — Fiction.   2.   Brothers and sisters — Fiction.]
I. Stevenson, Suçie, ill.   II. Title.
PZ7.W78032Do   1990
[E] — dc19   88-37109
                                                          CIP
                                                           AC

10 9 8 7 6 5 4 3 2 1

WOR

Published simultaneously in Canada
by Little, Brown & Company (Canada) Limited

Printed in the United States of America

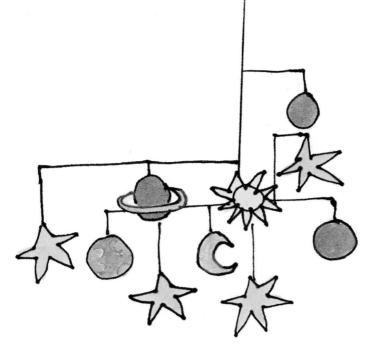

To David and Suzie, who share something special

F. W.

To Janet Burke and Asa

S. S.

Nobody could make Baby Louise stop crying.

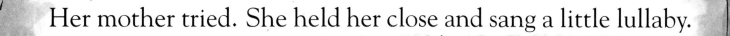

Her mother tried. She held her close and sang a little lullaby.

But that didn't help.

Louise kept on crying till her tears ran like rivers to the sea.

Her father tried. He rocked her gently in his arms and whispered softly in her ear.

But that didn't help.

Louise kept on crying till her wails shook the pictures off the walls.

Grandma tried. She gave her a nice warm bottle and said, "Eat. Eat."

But that didn't help.

Louise kept on crying till her sobs woke all the dogs and cats on the block.

Grandpa tried. He played a happy tune on his harmonica and did a little jig.

But that didn't help.

Louise kept on crying till the birds flew out of the trees
and the squirrels scampered away.

The neighbors came and offered advice.

"Turn her on her stomach."

"Turn her on her back."

"Change her diaper."

"Play Mozart."

"Play rock and roll."

But nothing helped.

Louise kept on crying.

Then, her brother, Daniel, came home from school.
"Oonga Boonga," he said to Louise.
Louise looked up, tears still streaming down her face.

"Oonga Boonga," he repeated.

Louise stopped sobbing and looked him straight in the eye.

"Oonga Boonga," said Daniel again.

Louise broke into a smile.

"How did you do that?" asked his mother.
"It's easy. You just say Oonga Boonga," said Daniel.

"Oonga Boonga," said his mother.

"Oonga Boonga," said his father.

"Oonga Boonga," said Grandma and Grandpa.

"See," said Daniel, "she likes it."

And sure enough, she did. Louise was smiling from ear to ear.

"Oonga Boonga," said everyone in unison.

"I'm going out to play," said Daniel.
"Be back at six for dinner," said his mom.

But as soon as he left, Louise's smile faded. Slowly a tear rolled down her cheek, followed by another, and then another.

And soon she was crying as loudly as before.

"Oonga Boonga," said her mother.

"Oonga Boonga," said her father.

"Oonga Boonga," said Grandma and Grandpa.

But nothing helped. Louise kept on crying.
"I think she wants Daniel," said her mother.

"Here I am," said Daniel.
Then he leaned over and whispered,

"Bonka Wonka, Louise."

And, to no one's surprise, Louise stopped crying.